This Book belong To

Adejare Adelowo

St Anthony's Catholic

Primary School.

CLASS ST. FRANCIS

Topsy + Tim

go to the dentist

Jean and Gareth Adamson

Published by Ladybird Books Ltd
27 Wrights Lane London W8 5TZ
A Penguin Company
3 5 7 9 10 8 6 4
© Jean and Gareth Adamson MCMXCV
This edition MCMXCVIII

Printed in Italy

It was time for Topsy and Tim
to visit the dentist. Mummy took
them to see Mrs Berry, the dentist
at the Health Centre. They sat in
the waiting room and read comics.

The dentist's door opened and out
came Josie Miller and her mummy.
Josie smiled at Topsy and Tim.
'I've got to wear a brace on
my teeth,' she said.
'Why?' asked Topsy.
'To make my teeth grow straight,'
said Josie.
'Mrs Berry is ready to see you now,
Topsy and Tim,' said the nurse.

'Hello twins,' said Mrs Berry.
'Your surgery smells funny!' said Topsy.
'It's a nice clean smell,' said Mummy.

'Who wants to go first?' said Mrs Berry.
'ME!' said Tim. He climbed into
the dentist's chair.
Mrs Berry pressed a button
and the chair tilted back.
Tim felt like a rocket pilot.
Mrs Berry put a disposable mask
over her nose and mouth.
'What's that for?' asked Tim.
'So that I don't breathe over you,'
said Mrs Berry.

'Open wide and let me see your teeth,'
said Mrs Berry.
Tim opened his mouth as wide as he could.
'This small mirror will help me
look for holes in Tim's teeth,'
said Mrs Berry. 'Little holes can
turn into big holes and big holes
can turn into toothache!'

There were no little holes in Tim's teeth.

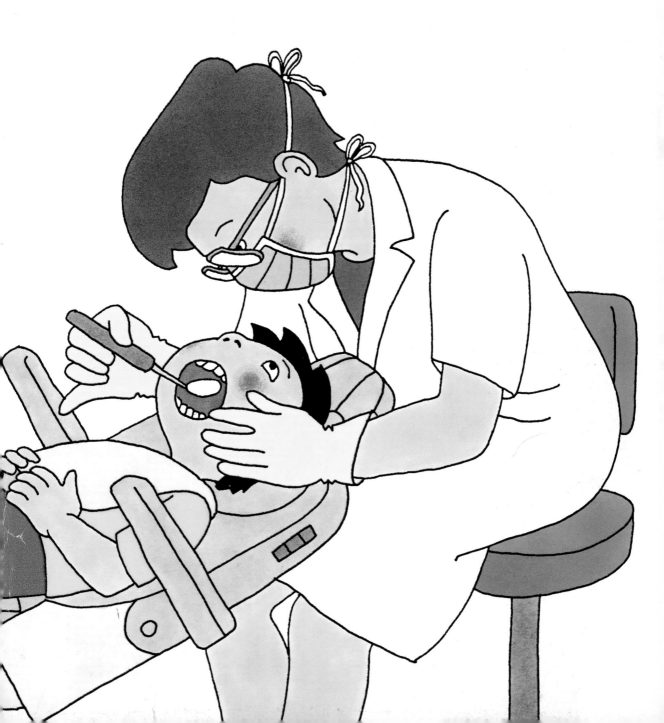

'Your turn now, Topsy,' said Mrs Berry.
She found a little hole in one of
Topsy's teeth.
'I'll clean that hole and put
a filling in it,' said Mrs Berry.
'It will stop pieces of food getting
in and turning nasty.'
First Mrs Berry hung a sucking
tube in Topsy's mouth.
'That's to stop you dribbling,'
she said. The tube made
funny sucking noises.
Then she used her whizzy
drill to clean out the hole
in Topsy's tooth.

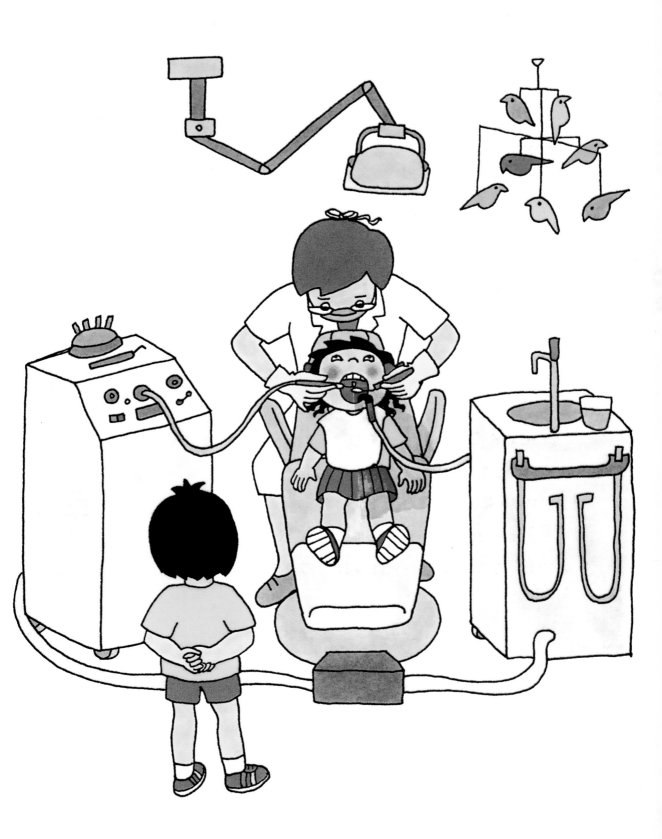

The nurse gave Topsy a glass
of pink water to rinse her mouth.
Then Mrs Berry dried the hole
with a little air blower,
so that the filling would stick
tight inside it.

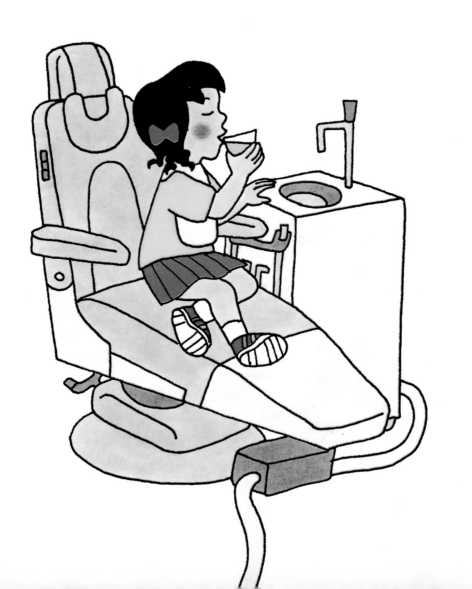

The nurse mixed a tiny bit of
silver filling. Tim watched her.
'That's Topsy's filling,' she said.

Mrs Berry pushed
the silver filling into
the hole in Topsy's
tooth. She pressed
it down and made
it perfectly smooth.

'There! Good as new!' said Mrs Berry.
'Did it hurt?' asked Tim.
'The drill was noisy,' said Topsy.
'But it didn't hurt.'

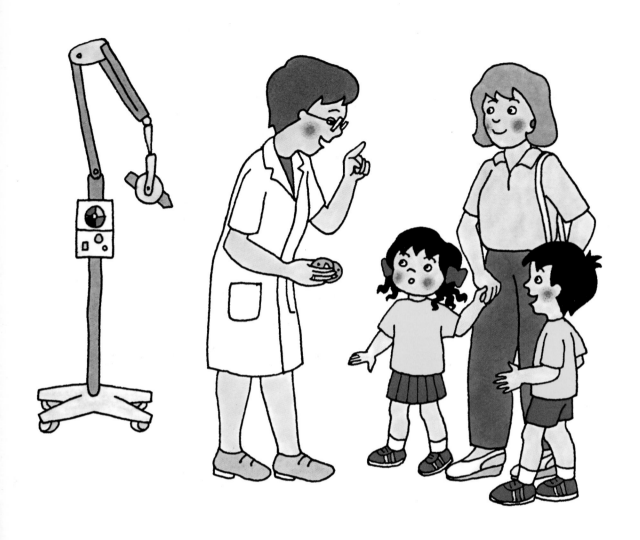

'You've both got good teeth,' said
Mrs Berry. 'Keep them that way.
Eat lots of different foods but remember,
sweet foods can hurt your teeth,
so don't eat them too often.

Never forget to clean your teeth
in the morning and at bedtime
and don't eat or drink in bed.'
'Not even water?' said Tim.
'Only water,' said Mrs Berry.
'Sweet drinks can hurt your teeth
as much as sweet food.'
Mrs Berry gave Topsy and Tim
a badge each to remind them
to look after their teeth.
'Come back and see me soon,' she said.

Before they went home the receptionist
wrote down the date of their next visit.
A little boy came into the waiting
room with his mummy. He was trying
not to cry.
'It's Tony Welch,' said Topsy.

'What's the matter, Tony?' asked Tim.
'I've got toothache,' sniffed Tony.
'He eats too many sweets,' said
Tony's mum.
'Never mind,' said Topsy. 'Mrs Berry
will make it better.'

On the way home they passed a sweet shop.
'I would like some sweets,' said Topsy,
'but I don't want toothache like Tony.'

'There are other nice things that are better for you,' said Mummy. She bought them lovely crunchy apples from the greengrocer.

Then they went to the chemist
to buy new toothbrushes.
The chemist told them about
disclosing tablets.
'Just chew half a tablet, then
rinse your mouth with water,'
he explained. 'The parts of your
teeth that most need cleaning
will turn pink.'

'We'd look funny going to school
with pink teeth,' said Tim.
The chemist laughed. 'You
clean away the pink bits with
your new toothbrushes,' he said.
'When there is no pink left,
you know your teeth are clean.'

As soon as they got home Topsy
and Tim tried out their new
toothbrushes.
'Mrs Berry won't find any holes
in our teeth next visit,' said
Topsy to Tim.